BIG BIRD
Goes to the Doctor

By TISH SOMMERS · Illustrated by TOM COOKE

CTW
SESAME STREET
A GROWING-UP BOOK™

Featuring Jim Henson's Sesame Street Muppets

On *Sesame Street* David is played by Northern Calloway.

A SESAME STREET / GOLDEN PRESS BOOK
Published by Western Publishing Company, Inc. in conjunction with Children's Television Workshop.

It was a beautiful day on Sesame Street. Grover was showing everyone his new tricycle.

"Be careful, Grover," said Ernie. "Don't go too fast!"

"Watch out!" yelled Oscar. "You almost ran over my pet worm, Slimey!"

"Oh, my goodness!" cried Grover as he wheeled around the trash can and almost ran into Big Bird.

"Good morning, everybody." Granny Bird came
hurrying down Sesame Street. "Have you seen Big Bird?
It's time for us to go to the doctor."

Big Bird hid behind the lamppost. Going for a
checkup was not one of his favorite things.

"Oh, I don't need a checkup today," Big Bird told Granny. "I feel fine."

"I know you're not sick," said Granny, "but once a year the doctor must examine you and see how much you weigh and how tall you've grown."

"If we wait until next year, I'll be even taller," said Big Bird.

"Come on, Big Bird," said Granny.

On the way to the doctor's office, Big Bird thought of something else.

"Will I have to get a shot?" he asked.

"I don't know," said Granny. "We'll see what the doctor says. But if you do, it will only hurt for a minute."

Big Bird wasn't so sure.

When they got to the doctor's office, Herry Monster was just leaving. He was pushing his baby sister, Flossie, in a baby-monster carriage.

"Hi, Herry," said Big Bird. "Is Flossie sick?"

"No," said Herry. "She just had her checkup and she's fine."

"Did it hurt?" Big Bird asked, but Flossie was too little to answer.

Big Bird and Granny sat down in the doctor's waiting room. Two kids were building with blocks, and others were looking at picture books. Some children didn't feel like playing.

"Do you want to help me with my puzzle?" asked Prairie Dawn.

"Sure," said Big Bird. He didn't hear Nurse Nightingale until the second time she called him.

"You're next, Big Bird," she said. "You and your granny can come in now."

"Please take off your clothes now, Big Bird," the nurse said. So far, she had seen six children, two furry monsters, and one Twiddlebug. "I forgot," she said. "You have feathers instead."

"That's all right," said Big Bird. "Everyone makes mistakes."

Granny sat down in the corner.

Just then Dr. Staywell came in. "Hello, Big Bird," she said. "How are you feeling?"

"Fine," said Big Bird in a tiny squeak.

The doctor sat down and opened a folder with Big Bird's name on it. "Have you been eating well?" she asked.

"Oh, yes," said Big Bird. "I eat three meals a day and have one birdseed milk shake for a snack."

"Have you been sleeping well?" asked the doctor.

"Yes, I'm snug in my nest every night at eight o'clock," answered Big Bird.

The doctor asked him a few more questions, and wrote carefully on Big Bird's chart.

"Excuse me, Doctor," said Nurse Nightingale. "There is a furry blue monster out here who fell off his tricycle and hurt his arm."

"Oh, my goodness!" said the doctor. "Tell Grover I'll be right there."

She turned to Big Bird. "I'll be back in a few minutes. The nurse will weigh and measure you now."

"Let's see how tall you are," said Nurse Nightingale.

Big Bird stood on the scale. "Eight feet, two inches!"

"Wow!" said Big Bird. "I've grown seven inches since last year."

The nurse moved the weights across the top of the scale. "152 pounds!"

"The biggest kid I've ever seen," she said to herself.

When Dr. Staywell returned she told them that Grover would be fine.

"Now, Big Bird," she said, "open your beak so that I can look at your throat."

Big Bird opened wide. Dr. Staywell shined a little flashlight into his throat and pushed his tongue down gently with a flat wooden stick.

"Ahhhh…" said Big Bird.

She shined another **flashlight** into Big Bird's ears. They weren't easy to find under all his feathers.

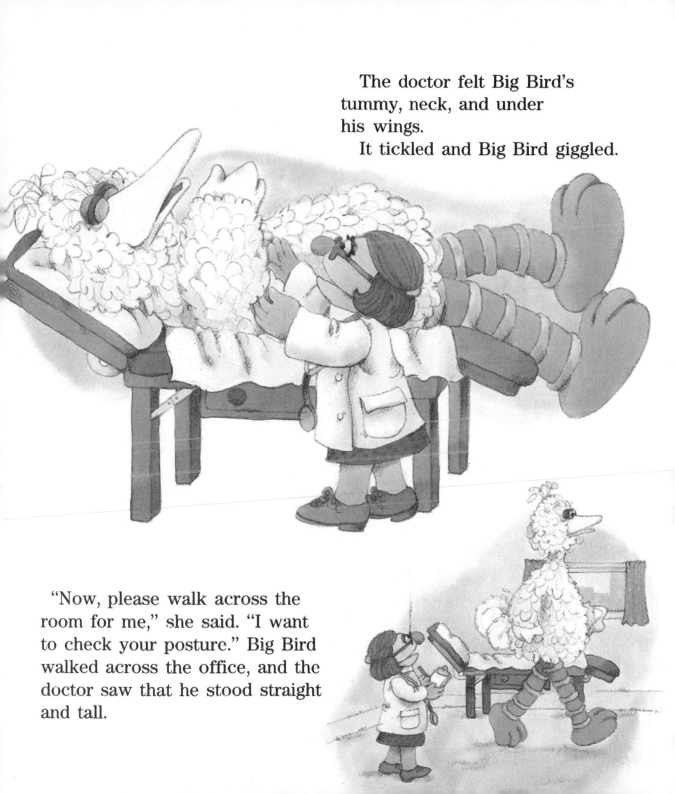

The doctor felt Big Bird's
tummy, neck, and under
his wings.
It tickled and Big Bird giggled.

"Now, please walk across the
room for me," she said. "I want
to check your posture." Big Bird
walked across the office, and the
doctor saw that he stood straight
and tall.

The doctor put a stethoscope
on Big Bird's chest and listened
to his heart. She let Big Bird
listen, too. He heard his heart
go *ka-thump ka-thump*.

She took his temperature with a thermometer.

"98.6," she said. "That's normal."

Dr. Staywell tapped Big Bird's knee with a small rubber hammer, and it made his leg jerk forward. "You have very **good** reflexes," she told him.

"Thank you," said Big Bird politely. He wasn't sure what reflexes were, but it sounded like a compliment.

"Now I'm going to check your eyes," Dr. Staywell told Big Bird. "Do you know your alphabet?"

"Oh, yes," he said proudly. "B is my favorite letter because I have two B's in my name."

"Well, cover one eye with your hand and read all the letters on the chart," said the doctor.

Big Bird read all the letters, especially the B's, in a clear, loud voice.

"Very good," said the doctor.

"That was fun," said Big Bird. "Am I done now?"

"Doctor," said Nurse Nightingale, "there's a shaggy blue monster with big, googly eyes out here who has a stomachache. He says he ate a whole box of chocolate cuppycakes…"

"Tell Cookie Monster I'll be right there," the doctor said. "Big Bird and I are almost finished."

The doctor smiled at Big Bird. "You are a very healthy bird," she told him. "There's just one more thing. Your chart shows that you should have a shot."

"Maybe some other time," said Big Bird. "Thanks anyway."

"Big Bird," said Granny, "you must have a shot now to keep you from getting sick."

"Will it hurt?" he asked.

"Only for a minute," said the doctor.

Granny put her arm around Big Bird, and the doctor held his wing and quickly gave him the shot. "See, that wasn't so bad, was it?" the doctor asked. "You were very brave."

The doctor put a small, round band-aid over the spot.

"Good-by, Big Bird," said Dr. Staywell. "Stay well and you won't have to visit me until your next checkup!"

"Thank you, Doctor," said Big Bird. "I'll see you next year!"

"Here's a balloon for you," said the nurse, "and one for Grover, and one for Cookie Monster."

"Thank you, Nurse Nightingale," they said. "So long!"

"How's your arm?" Big Bird asked Grover as they left the doctor's office.

"It is only a sprain," said Grover. "I will be back on my tricycle in a few days. But I promised the doctor to be more careful."

Big Bird, Granny, Grover, and Cookie Monster headed back to Sesame Street.

"How did it go at the doctor's office?" asked David when they walked into Hooper's Store.

"Fine," said Big Bird. "The doctor looked at my throat and my ears and watched me walk around, and I listened to my heart and read the alphabet. Then I got a shot and it only hurt for a minute." He showed David the band-aid on his wing.

"And my arm feels better already," said Grover.

"Two cuppycakes, please," said Cookie Monster.